# Caught Blue-Handed

By Sheila Sweeny Higginson
Based on the episode written by Kent Redeker
Illustrated by Alan Batson

**ABDOBOOKS.COM**

Reinforced library bound edition published in 2019 by Spotlight, a division of ABDO, PO Box 398166, Minneapolis, Minnesota 55439. Spotlight produces high-quality reinforced library bound editions for schools and libraries. Published by agreement with Disney Press, an imprint of Disney Book Group.

Printed in the United States of America, North Mankato, Minnesota.
092018      012019

**DISNEY PRESS**
New York • Los Angeles

THIS BOOK CONTAINS
RECYCLED MATERIALS

Library of Congress Control Number: 2017961153

Publisher's Cataloging-in-Publication Data

Names: Higginson, Sheila Sweeny, author. | Redeker, Kent, author. | Batson, Alan, illustrator.
Title: Doc McStuffins: Caught blue-handed / by Sheila Sweeny Higginson and Kent Redeker; illustrated by Alan Batson.
Description: Minneapolis, MN : Spotlight, 2019 | Series: World of reading level pre-1
Summary: When Chilly arrives in Doc's clinic covered in blue spots, Doc tracks down the reason for this case of "Mystery Pox."
Identifiers: ISBN 9781532141775 (lib. bdg.)
Subjects: LCSH: Doc McStuffins (Television program)--Juvenile fiction. | Toys--Juvenile fiction. | Germs--Juvenile fiction. | Spread of communicable diseases--Juvenile fiction. | Readers (Primary)--Juvenile fiction.
Classification: DDC [E] dc23

**Spotlight**
A Division of ABDO
abdobooks.com

 wants to show  the
painting he made.
"Guess what it is, ," he says
to his sister.

Donny

Doc

Doc

2

 looks at the painting.
Doc

She does not know what it is.

"It's a blue  eating !"
            elephant              blueberries

says .
     Donny

3

Donny runs inside to show Mom.
Doc's stethoscope begins to glow.
Her toys come to life like magic!

Her toy friends want to say hello.

Lambie jumps up and gives  Doc a cuddle.

"It's baa-baa-beautiful to see you!"  Lambie says.

 toy wants to say hi, too.

He has six .
hands

"Hiya, !" says  toy.
Doc                    Donny's

"Hi, !" says .
Glo-Bo              Doc

 hops up and gives
Squeakers                          Glo-Bo
a high five.

"What's squeaking with my

friend?"  asks.
          Glo-Bo

 pats  on the back.
Glo-Bo          Surfer Girl
"How's the surf?" he asks.
"Up!"  says.
          Surfer Girl

Next,  plays with  the
Glo-Bo                                    Buddy

dump truck.

Then he gives  a big bear hug.
Chilly

That is one tight squeeze!

Then  runs back to the
Glo-Bo

painting 🪑.
table

"I think I broke a ," says.

laughs. "Snowmen don't have bones!"

bone    Chilly

Doc

11

 doesn't have a broken .
Chilly                                        bone

But there is something wrong.

He has spots!

"
Chilly
, you need a checkup,"
says
Doc
.
Doc
McStuffins will make
Chilly
feel better!

 looks in Chilly's .

Doc                            mouth

She checks  .

Chilly's  eyes

 listens to Chilly's .

Doc                               heart

 uses a 🌡 to take ⛄ temperature.
Doc               thermometer       Chilly's

"You don't have a fever, ⛄," says 👧.
                              Chilly                Doc

"That's good."

15

"I have a diagnosis," says .
Doc

" has blue spots on his back.
Chilly
He has a case of mystery pox."

16

"Mystery pox?"  cries. "I don't know what mystery pox is!"

"Nobody does," Doc says. "That's why it's a mystery."

comes into  office with

Hallie     Doc's

more patients.

 has blue spots.

Squeakers

 and  have blue spots, too.

Buddy     Surfer Girl

"This is horrible!" says  .
Chilly

Then he holds his head and faints.

 steps in to catch .

Hallie                        Chilly

Now  has blue spots, too!

Hallie

 knows how the mystery pox

Doc

is spreading now.

20

Lambie wants to cuddle Chilly.

"Don't cuddle Chilly!" says Doc.

"You might get mystery pox, too!"

"Is it the end of cuddles?" Lambie asks.

 tells  why she can't cuddle.

Doc    Lambie

The pox is spreading.

It is like the germs that can make

people sick.

Now  has to find out who
started spreading the mystery pox.

Hallie got the mystery pox after she touched Chilly.

24

" **Chilly**, who else might have touched you?" **Doc** asks.

Chilly remembers something.

" Glo-Bo gave me a big hug!" he says.

26

" patted my back!" says .
Glo-Bo                          Surfer Girl

"Me, too!"  adds.
Buddy

"That's it!" says . She runs to the
Doc

yard to find .
Glo-Bo

27

 finds . He is about to
Doc          Glo-Bo

hug .
      Teddy B

"Stop!" she yells. "I think you're

spreading mystery pox."

28

takes a close look at .

Doc

Glo-Bo

He is not sick.

But  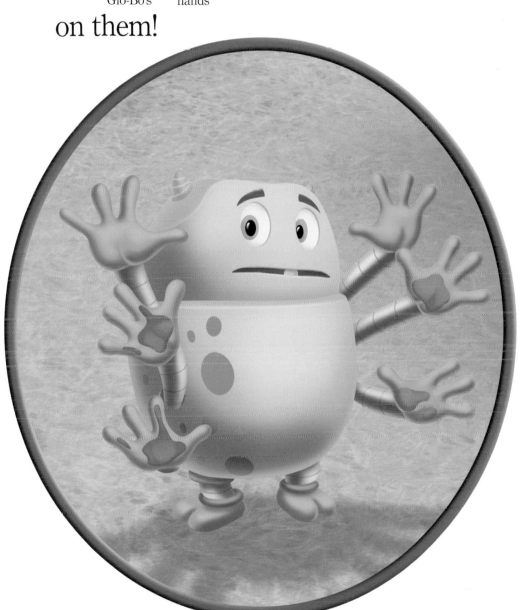 have blue paint

Glo-Bo's     hands

on them!

"It's not mystery pox,"  says.
Doc

"It's blue paint from Glo-Bo's hands!"

"Phew!" says Chilly.

Everyone goes back to Doc's clinic.

The hand-washing party begins!  washes , , and .

Doc          Glo-Bo  Chilly          Squeakers

Then she washes , , and .

Buddy  Surfer Girl          Hallie

No more mystery pox!

has one last question.

Did you wash your  today?

hands